I'M JAY, LET'S PLAY

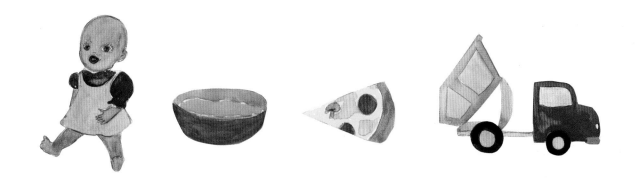

By Beth Reichmuth

Illustrated by Nomy Lamm

First U.S. edition 2016.

ISBN 978–0–692–79767–9

Printed in Malaysia by TWP Sdn. Bhd.

Design by Sophie Argetsinger.

Special thanks to Laura Lifland for the support, inspiration and encouragement at every step. Thank you to my amazing colleagues for your invaluable insights and edits—especially Jessica Moskowitz, Melodie Younce, Lisa Treadway, Tim Treadway, and Leslie Roffman.

Thank you to all of the folks who backed this book through our crowd funding campaign. *I'm Jay Let's Play* would not exist without you.

I offer this book with love, respect, and gratitude for transgender, non-binary, and queer activists—who, for generations, have been doing the important work of creating safe spaces that respect and celebrate gender-creative youth.

—B.R.

For the original Jay, because it's fun to feel seen and celebrated.

—B.R.

May we all find opportunities to engage our wild
and squiggly selves in a spirit of creation.

—N.L.

I'm Jay. This is my preschool.

There are so many fun things to do.
But what I like to do very best is play with my friends!

Me and Ren love playing restaurant, so we cook pizza. Yum it's tasty!

We pile it up on dump trucks and drive off.
"Pizza for sale!" we yell. "Who wants pizza?"

Finn is playing family.
"Oooh, my babies love pizza! And they need lunch!" Finn cries.

"If the babies are hungry, we have to stop!" I say.
I dump the whole truckload. "Beep, beep, beep! Here ya go."
"Oh, no!" Ren shouts, "Those babies ate all the pizza!"

We drive as fast as rockets back to the kitchen.

This time we make soup. It's fresh, hot, and ready to share!

It's a good thing too, 'cause I see friends who are going to be hungry.

Casey and Riley are construction workers. They built a super tall tower. "Don't worry workers, lunch is on the way!" I call.

Our soup is so tasty that they eat it all up.
"Wow, this tower is SO huge," says Ren.
"Yeah, even bigger than me!" I agree.

"Hey," says Casey, "it looks like the light is shining from your skirt."
"It's the sparkles!" I say. "Watch me spin."
"Wow, I wish I had a skirt like that!" Casey whispers.

Then I remember something. It's the perfect idea.
"Follow me, Casey. I have a little surprise for you…"

I unzip my backpack. I pull out something really special …

It's another skirt just the same as mine!
Casey puts it right on. "Same, same!" we both say. We laugh and laugh.

We look so fancy! Fancy for a party.
We invite all our friends to an extra-fancy pizza and soup party.

First stop, though? Dress-up corner!

We skip and twirl to the restaurant.

We eat pizza, soup, watermelon, carrots, and pickles.
We even have my favorite dessert—cupcakes! It's the best party ever.

Ding! Ding! Ding! I know what that sound means.
Only five more minutes until clean up time.

"Wait! What about our tower?" Casey asks.
"Oooh, let's knock it down!" yells Riley.

The whole party heads over to the construction site.

The tower falls over big time.

Blocks are everywhere. All the kids are laughing now!

"Time to clean up, friends!" our teacher sings.

Now that was a fun morning at school!

Dear Reader,

Here are some phrases that I find useful when reading and discussing *I'm Jay, Let's Play* with children:

- I don't know if _____ feels like a boy or a girl, but they seem like a really fun friend. I notice they like to play with _____, just like you and your friends do.

- All clothes and all toys are for everyone who likes them. Sparkly skirts are for everyone. Superheroes are for everyone. Pink is for everyone. Dinosaurs are for everyone. What else is for everyone?

- Sometimes people think some things are just for boys, and other things are just for girls. But that's not true. We should all get to pick what we like.

- There are lots of ways to be a boy. There are lots of ways to be a girl. It is okay to feel like neither or both or something else.

- What's most important about being a girl, or a boy, or something else is how you feel inside. That is something we each get to explore for ourselves.

Thank you for your presence and thoughtfulness with children. I know that together we can make our communities safer, sweeter, and more celebratory spaces for all of us.

Warmly,

Beth

We should all be able to wear what helps us feel joyful, powerful, playful, proud, or whole.

Sparkly skirts are for everyone who likes them.

Sparkly skirts are for John.

Sparkly skirts are for Luna and Siena.

Sparkly skirts are for Adeline, and Billy, and Philip.

Sparkly skirts are for Anika.

Sparkly skirts are for Boon.

Sparkly skirts are for Timoteo.

Sparkly skirts are for Elsie, Auntie Haley, Auntie Steph, and Mabel.

Sparkly skirts are for Earnest.

Sparkly skirts are for John, and Beck, and Johnny, and Carley.

Sparkly skirts are for Piper and Phoebe.

Sparkly skirts are for Angie, and Peter, and Parker.

Sparkly skirts are for Lucas.

Sparkly skirts are for Mishca, and Lamby, and Ima, and all the pets.

Sparkly skirts are for Hayden, and Lexington, and Heather, and Darcy.

Sparkly skirts are for Josie and Roque.

Sparkly skirts are for Ivy.

Sparkly skirts are for you if you like them!